OUT OF THE ASHES

Michael Morpurgo

Illustrations by Michael Foreman

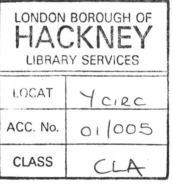

G·A·L·A·X·Y CHILDREN'S·LARGE·PRINT

Galaxy

CHIVERS PRESS
BATH

First published 2001
by
Macmillan Children's Books
This Large Print edition published by
Chivers Press
by arrangement with
Macmillan Children's Books
2002

ISBN 0 7540 6190 6

British Library Cataloguing in Publication Data

Morpurgo, Michael
Out of the ashes.—Large print ed.
1. Foot-and-mouth disease—England—Devon—Juvenile fiction. 2. Farm life—England—Devon—Juvenile fiction. 3. Children's stories. 4. Large type books
I. Title II. Foreman, Michael. 1938–
823.9'14[J]

ISBN 0-7540-6190-6

Printed and bound in Great Britain by
BOOKCRAFT, Midsomer Norton, Somerset

Supporting Farmers in Crisis Fund

The rural areas of Britain have never known anything quite like the foot and mouth epidemic of 2001. So grievous was the injury and so great the shock, that thousands of farming families and sometimes whole communities have been traumatized. At the time of writing, in early June, more than three million animals have been slaughtered on 7,900 farms. That is nearly eight times more animals killed than during the 1967/68 outbreak.

What *Out of the Ashes* does supremely well and movingly is to bring home just what those impersonal statistics mean to real people, with real animals, on real farms.

From the moment that the extent of the crisis in the countryside became clear, donations came flooding in to the National Farmers' Union, from businesses, organizations and ordinary people. The NFU set up the Supporting Farmers in Crisis fund to make sure that help was given where it was most needed as quickly as possible—particularly in maintaining counselling services like the Farm Crisis Network, which has done invaluable work. The fund also aims to assist beyond the short term—in the process of rebirth and renewal in rural communities.

We are very grateful indeed that Michael Morpurgo's publishers are making a generous donation to the Fund. Every penny will be well and wisely used.

Anthony Gibson
National Farmers' Union

This book is dedicated to all those farmers and farming communities who suffered during the foot and mouth outbreak of 2001.

An introduction I want you to read

This story is not a story at all. It all happened. I know it did because I was there. I lived it. I saw it with my own eyes. It was a time of my life I can never forget.

I wrote it just as a private diary. Dad gave me a lovely leather-bound diary for my thirteenth birthday last year. It's peacock blue with a brass clip. I'm one of those few unlucky people whose birthday falls on Christmas Day, so whilst I might not get as many presents as my friends, mine are usually very special. And this was my most special present of all last year, mostly because Dad had had my name, Becky Morley, printed in gold on the front, and underneath, 'My diary 2001.' And best of all, he'd done a drawing on the first page of Ruby—Ruby's my horse. She's bay, with a dark mane and tail, part Connemara, part thoroughbred. I used to think she was the most important thing in the world to me. Below the drawing Dad had written 'Ruby, the only one who's allowed to read this—except Becky. Love Dad.' It was a wonderful drawing too—Ruby at full gallop. It's always amazed me how well Dad can draw. He's got great big farmer's hands, like spades, and yet he draws a lot better than me, better than anyone I know.

From January 1st 2001 onwards, I wrote something in my diary about once a week, sometimes more. I could write as little or as much as I wanted, because the pages weren't dated, no saints' days, no holidays, just empty pages. So I could do drawings too, when I felt like it. My diary year, like everyone else's, began on January 1st, but it ended on April 30th, because the story was over. There just didn't seem any point in writing any more.

Some time afterwards, I showed it to Mum. After all we'd been through together I wanted her to read it. Once she'd finished she gave me a long hug, and we cried our last tears. At that moment I felt we had both drawn a line under the whole thing and made an end of it.

It was her idea, not mine, that my diary should be published. She was very determined about it, fierce almost. 'People should know, Becky,' she said. 'I want people to know how it was. I certainly don't want their pity, but I do want them to understand.'

So here's my diary, then, with some of my drawings too. Not a word has been changed. The spelling has been corrected, and the punctuation. Otherwise it's just as I wrote it.

'Ruby, the only one who's allowed to read this—except Becky. Love, Dad.'

MONDAY, JANUARY 1ST

Dad was a bit bleary-eyed this morning. After last night I'm not surprised. We were up at the Duke of York seeing the New Year in, along with most of the village—Jay, Uncle Mark, Auntie Liz, everyone—the place was packed.

But New Year 2001 for us didn't begin in the pub. I stood with Mum in the dark of the church and watched Dad and the others ringing in the New Year. He's a lot bigger than all the other bell ringers, and he rings the bell with the deepest dong. It suits him.

Afterwards, in the cold night air we all tramped through the graveyard to join the party at the Duke. An owl hooted from up in the church tower, and Dad called out: 'And a Happy New Year to you too!'

Dad was laughing a lot like he always does, and drinking too, but no more than anyone else. Mum kept telling him that he'd had enough and that he'd only have a thick head in the morning.

I hate it when she nags him like that, especially in front of other people. But Dad didn't seem to mind at all. I think he was too happy to care. He was singing his heart out. He sang 'Danny Boy' and everybody cheered him. He loves to sing when he's happy. Everyone was happy last night, including me. Jay and me went outside when the pub got too stuffy and smoky and we lay on the village green looking up at the stars. It was cold, but we didn't mind. The owl kept hooting at us from the graveyard. Jay said she saw a shooting star, but she was just making it up. She's always making things up, particularly what she calls her 'experiences' about boys, and sometimes that makes me annoyed because I think she's trying to put me down. But last night she was just having fun. I feel she is more like my sister than my best friend. I know her so well, too well probably.

Jay was beside me later on when we all linked arms and sang 'Auld Lang Syne' (I can never remember the words) before we went back home in the pick-up, Bobs in the back, barking his head off at the moon. He always barks and howls on moonlit nights—'like a ruddy werewolf,' Dad says.

When we got back I went to see Ruby in her stable to wish her a Happy New Year. I gave her lots of sugar lumps and a kiss on her nose. Then I did the same to Bobs so he didn't feel left out—not sugar lumps, just a kiss. When I got up to bed Dad was already snoring, as loud as a chainsaw.

This afternoon I took Ruby for a ride. Bobs came along. Bobs always comes along. Up through Bluebell Wood and down to the river. Two herons lifted off as we cantered across the water meadows. Love herons. The river was low enough, so I rode Ruby across into Mr Bailey's wood the other side. Bobs had to swim, paddling like crazy, head up and looking very pleased with himself. We've got this brilliant arrangement with Mr Bailey. He lets me ride in his woods and in return I let him have horse manure for his vegetable garden. Unlike us, he keeps the tracks through his woods clear; so, as long as I look out for badger holes, I can let Ruby have her head. She galloped on well today, puffing and snorting like she does when she's really enjoying herself.

As I came out of the wood I saw Mr Bailey feeding his sheep. He waved at me and called out, wishing me a Happy New Year, which surprised me because

he can be a bit grumpy. (He wasn't in the pub last night. He's a Methodist. He doesn't like pubs.) Normally we only wave at each other at a distance. So I rode over to say hello, just to be friendly. He told me he'd be lambing down his ewes in a week or so (he calls them 'yors'). 'Don't want any snow,' he said. 'Worst thing you can have at

lambing time is snow.'

Then he asked me if I'd made any New Year's resolutions, and I said I hadn't. 'You should, Becky,' he told me. 'I always do. I don't always keep them, mind. But I try. And trying's what counts.' So I thought about it on the way back home, and I made two New Year's resolutions. First: to write in my diary like I'm doing now every single day. Second: to be nicer to Mum, if she'll be nicer to me.

THURSDAY, JANUARY 11TH

Both my New Year's resolutions have been broken. It's ten days since I wrote a word in my diary, and Mum and I still aren't getting on at all. Now come my excuses. I didn't write in my diary partly because I couldn't think of anything much to write about, and partly because Mum kept on pestering me to do it. She kept saying it would be good practice for my English (that's her trouble, she can't stop being a teacher) and that Dad would be disappointed if I didn't write in it every day. She pesters me about everything, not just about my diary.

Here's a list of my terrible crimes:

1. I haven't written my thank you letters for my Christmas/birthday presents. I'm doing it.
2. I left Ruby's gate unlatched and she got out. Once. By accident.
3. I still haven't tidied my room. So?
4. I take long showers and use up too

much water. I like showers.

5. I forgot to take my wellies off—once—when I came in off the farm. I was in a hurry to go to the loo.
6. I should spend less time with Ruby and more time on my homework—if I want 'to get on in life'.

What she doesn't understand is how much I love Ruby. Dad understands. He's the same about his cows and his pigs and the sheep. He loves them to bits. He's got twenty-five Gloucester cows and he knows them all by name—so do I. He names them all after flowers: Marigold, Tulip, Rose, Celandine. The boss cow is called Primrose. Primrose is always the first into the milking parlour, the first through every gate. She's got dreamy eyes and great curved horns. Dad loves her a lot—he's always slipping her sneaky peppermints.

In his dairy Dad makes the best cheese in the entire world—that's what he says and he's right. Double Gloucester, and it's the only Double Gloucester cheese made from Gloucester cows in the whole country. He's very proud of his cheese, very proud of his cows, and so am I. He's always in his dairy checking on his cheeses in the cheese store. Don't know why. Sometimes I think he just likes being with them.

But it's Hector Dad loves best, our old Gloucester bull. He was born on the farm twelve years ago, and he's so gentle you can lead him around with your little finger. Dad used to put me on his back when I was little—I've got a photo of it in my album.

Then we've got pigs—all 'J's, Jessica, Jemima and Jezebel. Black and white Gloucester Old Spots. There's three families at the moment, all different sizes of piglets and all very cute—except when they get into the garden and start digging up the lawn with their snouts. Just a couple of days ago Mum saw them out of the window at breakfast and went chasing after them with a broom. She was in her dressing gown and wellies. Dad nearly killed himself laughing and so did I.

Today I heard Mr Bailey's first lambs bleating from across the river. We haven't started lambing just yet.

That'll be in a couple of weeks' time. Dad wins prizes for his sheep—some Cotswolds, some Suffolks. We've got about a hundred and fifty in all. Like he does every year, he's picked me out three sheep of my own, my own flock—all Suffolks because he says they lamb easier. From now on I've got to look after them, and this year for the first time I've got to lamb them by myself when the time comes. I wrote out twenty names beginning with 'M' and chose the best three—Molly, Mary and May. Molly's the pushy one, and my favourite already.

I went back to school last week, last Monday. The heating broke down so we all froze. It was good seeing Jay and the others again, but I always find school strange at first. I'll get used to it. I always do. At the end of last term there were Christmas decorations up everywhere. Without them the school looks bare and empty, like the trees outside my window. They look like skeletons in winter. I'm fed up with this winter. It rains every day, which means the river's flooded and I can't cross over and go riding up in Mr Bailey's woods, and there's mud everywhere too. Ruby hates mud, and so do I. We agree on everything, Ruby and me.

Mrs Kennedy's away having her baby, so we've got a new English teacher, Mrs Merton. She told us all about herself. She's thirty-five, married with two children and grew up on a farm like me, and she smiles a lot. I like teachers who smile.

SATURDAY, JANUARY 20TH

Ruby's gone lame, and I'm sure it's because of all the mud. I've been leaving her out too long, because she hates being stuck in her stable all the time. Anyway, now she'll have to stay in, whether she likes it or not. The vet said so. 'Young MacDonald,' Dad calls him. (He's really good-looking, like Brad Pitt, and he wears an Australian hat.) So I call him Brad—when I'm thinking about him, which I do, often. He gave Ruby an injection and told me it wasn't my fault, but he was only saying that. It *was* my fault, I know it was. He took a look at my sheep in the shippen and told me they could be lambing any day now. He thought Molly might possibly be having twins. She is *so* big, so wide. 'Fine looking animals,' he said. 'I like to see well-kept stock, and there's no farmer round here that looks after his animals better than your dad.' Dad was right there behind him when he said it, and he was beaming all over his face.

'I bet you say that to all the farmers, don't you, young MacDonald?'

'Yep,' said Brad. And we all laughed then.

That was the moment I remember best today. I suddenly felt I wasn't younger than them at all, that I was one of them. Bobs chased Brad's car all the way up the road, as usual. He'll chase anything that moves, unless it's a farm animal. Dad says he's the laziest sheepdog he's ever had. But I think he's lovely—second only to Ruby in my heart. Maybe third. It's Ruby, then Brad, then Bobs. Sorry, Bobs.

At school Mrs Kennedy's had her baby—well, not at school exactly. It's a boy, and she's sent in a picture of him which Mrs Merton pinned up in the classroom. He's all wrinkled up and pink with his eyes tightly closed and his fists clenched. Mrs Merton got us to write about what he might be thinking behind his closed eyes. Jay wrote a long poem called: 'Thinking nothing' which was really good. And I wrote this whole story about the baby, dreaming of the life he'd had the last time he was alive, but I didn't have time to finish it before the bell went. I'll finish it another day.

Mum is thirty-eight today. We gave her her presents at breakfast as we always do on birthdays. I gave her a painting of Ruby I'd done at school with Bobs running along behind and she was really happy with it. I know that because when she thanked me her eyes were smiling at me, and because she didn't moan at me once all day.

They've gone out to dinner at The Duke to celebrate and Moody Trudy's here to babysit. I'm thirteen and they *still* think I need a babysitter. She's sitting on the sofa right now, crying her eyes out. (Who's babysitting who?) She's broken up with her boyfriend again. Always the same boyfriend, Terry Bolan, up at Speke's farm. She wants to get married, but he doesn't. I can't say I blame him. Trudy *is* moody, and I mean *really* moody.

Bobs is in the kitchen with me as I'm writing this. He keeps sighing and groaning in his basket. Trudy's still sniffling in the sitting room. I've had enough. I'm going out to talk to Ruby.

MONDAY, FEBRUARY 5TH

All good news. I got an 'A' for that story about Mrs Kennedy's baby's previous life. Mrs Merton wrote that it was a strange story, but very imaginative. I like her more and more. And better still, Ruby's foot is fine again. The vet came today, not Brad (pity!), another one, the one with a posh accent and a ginger moustache. He said I shouldn't ride her out for a while, just to be safe. *And*, *and*—I had my first lambs. Molly gave birth this morning before breakfast. I went out with Dad to check the lambing ewes—he's had twenty or so lambs already from his flock. We found Molly lying there in the corner of the shippen trying to do it by herself. She'd already given birth to one, but she was still struggling, still pushing. Brad had been right. There was a second one on the way. The head was already out. Dad didn't interfere. He held Molly still and just told me to get on with it. I'd helped him before and watched him dozens of times. I knelt down and pulled firmly, gently easing the lamb out.

It was hard at first because my hand kept slipping, and Molly seemed suddenly too tired to go on pushing. But then out came the lamb in one whoosh, and there he was lying on the straw. But he wasn't breathing. He was completely still. I panicked and wanted Dad to take over. But he just told me to keep calm, not to worry. Blow in his nostrils, he told me. So I did. Still the lamb didn't breathe. Then I had to hold him up by the back legs and give him a shake. 'Now lie him down and rub him,' Dad said. Suddenly the lamb began to splutter and cough and shake his head. I'd done it. All on my own (sort of). I'd given birth to my first lamb (sort of), a ram lamb (I love saying that out loud!). Dad checked Molly had plenty of milk, which she had.

Molly licked him all over and in half an hour he was up on his shaky legs, staggering around and nuzzling for his first drink. I've called him 'Little Josh' after Josh, my little cousin, because he's cute too, and because they have both got very short, curly black hair. So from now on I'd better call cousin Josh 'Big Josh', so I won't get the two of them muddled up.

I keep going out into the shippen to see if he's all right. He's learnt to walk, eat and talk, all in just a few hours. Amazing. He is so sweet and I'm so happy.

THURSDAY, FEBRUARY 15TH

All my lambs are born now. May lambed by herself last night. So, including Little Josh, I've got four lambs and they're all fine. Dad's just about finished, but what with all the milking and cheesemaking, as well as the lambing, he's very tired and stressed out. So Mum's helping, seeing to the sheep in the morning before she goes off to school, and then in the evening when she gets back. She does some milking for him too, at the weekends, just to give him a break. I'm doing the pigs and poultry before and after school. So we're all tired and fed up. At mealtimes we just eat in silence. That's the trouble with everyone being busy, it makes everyone very boring. No one even argues!

I can't ride Ruby yet, so I spend lots of time with Little Josh in the shippen. That's where I'm sitting writing this. Bobs isn't allowed in, in case he upsets the ewes. So he's sitting outside whining and sulking. He's just jealous. Here's a drawing of what I think I look like to Little Josh.

SATURDAY, FEBRUARY 24TH

Today I introduced Little Josh to Big Josh. Auntie Liz came for lunch along with all her family—first visitors we've had for a long time. I can't help it. I just look from Mum's face to Auntie Liz's and back again, looking for any differences. I've always done it. Identical twins, very identical. Identical to look at, but not in any other way. Auntie Liz is so quiet, and easygoing. I've felt bad about it all my life, but ever since I can remember I've wanted her to be my mother.

Uncle Mark and Dad get on really well together, like a couple of kids. They always go off shooting together or fishing, or maybe just down to the pub. Shooting today. Crows. They got eight. There's thousands of crows on the farm, and I hate them. They kill lambs. They'll even kill a sheep if they find one on its back. They peck out their eyes. No such thing as a nice crow.

Big Josh is six years old and he makes me laugh because he adores me. He wants to be with me all the time, holding my hand, sitting on my lap. And he's always asking if he can marry me. He asked me why I'd called him Little Josh. So I told him it was because Little Josh was cute and had curly black hair just like he did. He squealed with laughter and then picked Little Josh up in his arms and carried him everywhere. When Big Josh got tired he led him around on a piece of string like a puppy. Little Josh put up with it all, but he was as happy to see Molly again as Molly was to see him. Big Josh is lovely, but I was quite relieved to have the place to ourselves again when they all went off after tea.

I decided I'd waited long enough for Ruby's foot to heal, and that it was time to try her out again, gently. I had just about enough time to groom her, saddle her up, go for a short ride and get back before dark. Bobs came along with us and we went down to the river and crossed over. The river was still high after all the rain but we managed.

She went like a train up through Mr Bailey's woods and it was all I could do to rein her in at the top. She was puffing and blowing a bit, but I could tell there was nothing wrong with her foot. I was in amongst Mr Bailey's sheep and lambs before I knew it. They panicked and scattered everywhere. I just hoped Mr Bailey hadn't seen us.

By the time I'd got home, rubbed her down and fed her, it was dark. I kicked off my boots and called out that I was back. But no one said anything, and I thought that was strange because I knew they were in—I'd seen them through the window as I came past. When I went into the sitting room Mum and Dad were both sitting there just staring at a blank television

screen. Neither of them even turned to look at me. I knew they were upset about something. Then I thought that Mr Bailey must have rung up to complain about me scattering his sheep, that they were furious with me. But they said nothing, just sat there. I

asked what the matter was. Dad said it very quietly: 'Foot and mouth disease. Some pig farmer up north has got foot and mouth on his farm. It was on the news. They've had to kill thousands of pigs.'

I didn't know what he was on about. So Mum told me. It's a sort of virus that attacks farm animals—pigs, sheep, cows, and it spreads like wildfire. If you get it on your farm, then every animal has to be killed immediately to stop the disease from spreading. But it was nothing to worry about, she said, because the outbreak was over three hundred miles away and there was no way it could spread all the way down to us in Devon.

But I caught Dad's eye as she said that, and I could see he was worried. He tried to smile at me. 'We'll be all right, Becky,' he said, 'but all the same, I'm not taking any chances.'

From now on Dad says we've got to dip our wellies in disinfectant every time we come in and out of the house, and first thing tomorrow he's putting down a barrier of straw soaked in disinfectant at the farm gate, and a sign up saying 'Keep Out'. And we can't have any more visitors, not until the scare is over. Worst of all, he says I can't ride Ruby off the farm, just in case. He didn't say just in case of what and I didn't ask, because I didn't want it to sound like I was arguing. I don't like arguing with Dad because I know it hurts him when I do. So now I can't take Ruby galloping up in Mr Bailey's wood.

I'm writing this sitting in my bed, and I can hear them talking downstairs. I don't know why, because usually I love listening in to their conversations, but for some reason I just don't want to hear what they're saying.

P.S. Just after I finished writing this I suddenly thought of something dreadful. Ruby might get this foot and mouth thing. And Bobs. I ran downstairs and asked them straight out. Not possible, Mum said. The virus only attacks cloven-hoofed animals—pigs, cows and sheep. So Ruby's all right, and Bobs. But Little Josh isn't.

Nor is Molly, nor Hector, nor Primrose.

WEDNESDAY, FEBRUARY 28TH

Molly doesn't seem to have much milk of her own, just enough, Dad says, to feed one lamb, not two. So we've been feeding Little Josh on the bottle four times a day. I do it before school. Dad does it at lunchtime, because he's the only one at home, and I do it at teatime and then last thing before I go to bed. It's great, because Little Josh treats me like his mum now and follows me everywhere.

He followed me into the stable yesterday, and Ruby didn't like it at all. She put her ears back and tossed her head at him. Dad said I'd better shut Little Josh up, else the pigs might eat him. I can never be sure with Dad whether he's joking or not. But he's not been joking much recently. He's still worried sick about the case of foot and mouth disease on that farm up north.

There were pictures on the telly today of dead pigs being picked up by machines and laid on top of a great funeral pyre of railway sleepers and straw. It was horrible. They're burning them tomorrow. Mum keeps telling him there's no way that foot and mouth disease can spread all those hundreds of miles down to us. But Dad says you can never be sure of anything, not with foot and mouth disease, that it can spread on the wind, that it can get carried by people, by cars.

Internet, radio, television—he always wants to find out the latest news about it. And he's started smoking again. He gave up last year, for good he said. I went to help him in the dairy this evening, just to be with him. We milled the cheese together in silence. He didn't say so, but I knew he liked me being with him.

THURSDAY, MARCH 1ST

Some good news. Some bad news. The good news first. At school today Mrs Merton talked about foot and mouth disease. She said what Mum said, that foot and mouth isn't likely to find its way down here to us in Devon. Last time there was an outbreak, all the cases were clustered together in Shropshire. I told Dad when I came home, but I don't think he was even listening. And there's other farmers worried like he is. On the school bus, I've seen quite a few farms with disinfected straw mats across their farm gates, and there are more and more 'Keep Out' signs. Everywhere

you go now the air stinks of disinfectant. Ruby really hates it. She wrinkles up her nose whenever she smells it.

Now the bad news. I had a bust-up with Jay. I was just telling her how worried Dad was about the farm, and then she says that farmers are always moaning about something. And for no reason she goes on and on about how I had this and I had that and how I had a horse, and how I was spoilt—in front of everyone. And she's supposed to be my best friend. So I said *she* was spoilt because she's got the latest iMac computer—she's always showing it off to me when I go over to her place. Then she says if I feel like that she won't ever invite me over again. Well, who cares? God, she can be a right cow sometimes.

MONDAY, MARCH 5TH

Up until teatime it was a great day. At school Jay came and made it up. She said she'd been a real cow, and I said I liked cows. So we're best friends again.

Then I was sitting in the kitchen having my tea when Mum came in from work. She was white in the face and I soon knew why. They've discovered foot and mouth on a farm less than two miles away—on Speke Farm, Terry Bolan's place. She heard it on the radio in the car.

I'd never seen her so upset, and it wasn't just because of the foot and mouth. It was because she was going to have to tell Dad. He was still out on the farm somewhere. When we heard him coming she took my hand under the table and held it tight. Then she told him. It was like the life had suddenly gone out of him. All he said was: 'You sure?' Then, when Mum nodded, he just turned round and went out again. Mum went after him.

I haven't said a prayer since I gave up Sunday school a couple of years ago, until today. I sat at the kitchen table and prayed. I prayed that this foot and mouth wouldn't come to us, that our animals wouldn't catch it, that Little Josh wouldn't catch it, that everything would turn out all right. But then as I was praying I got angry, angry with God. Why did he let it happen? Why had he made it come here?

At supper I found out it wasn't God at all. Terry Bolan had bought in hundreds of sheep from a market up north, where that same pig farmer had sold his infected pigs before he knew they were infected. And the pigs had infected the sheep. Terry didn't know it. No one did. It wasn't his fault, Mum said. So God wasn't to blame, and nor was Terry. But the disease was here anyway, and now only two miles away from us.

Dad hardly ate anything at supper. He just sat there smoking and staring ahead of him. When I kissed him goodnight and hugged him just now, he hardly knew I'd done it. I'm going to pray again when I've finished writing this and I'm going to keep praying every night until I'm sure we won't get it.

Usually I do a drawing, but I can't, not tonight. I'm too sad.

TUESDAY, MARCH 6TH

Everything's still all right. So far. I didn't go to school today and Mum stayed at home too. No one in the village went to school in case we accidentally spread the foot and mouth infection. Mum says you can carry it in your hair and on your clothes, in your ears even and up your nose.

So I spent most of the morning out on the farm with Dad. I milked the cows with him, and then went off with him on the tractor checking every animal on the farm for any tell-tale sign of the disease. We were looking for any cow or pig or sheep with blisters or sores around the mouth, or in the feet. Dad said that I had to keep an eye out for any animal on its own, or limping, or that didn't look right in itself, and in particular any animal that was standing unnaturally still. When they've got blisters in the feet they don't like moving about because it hurts them, so they just stand still.

I must have been into the shippen and checked Little Josh and the others a dozen times today. Sometimes I just sat in the straw with them and watched them. I felt like a shepherd trying to keep a wolf away from my flock, except that this wolf is silent and invisible, and I can't frighten him off.

Dad has hardly said a word all day, and he didn't eat lunch and hardly any supper either. Mum is doing her best to cheer him up, and so am I, but foot and mouth is hanging over him like a dark shadow, and he hardly hears us. It's like he's cut himself off from us completely, like he's locked inside himself somehow and can't get out. I've never seen him like this before, and it frightens me.

WEDNESDAY, MARCH 7TH

It's bad news, not the worst, but nearly. The disease has come closer, much closer. We had a phone call at breakfast. Mr Bailey's sheep have caught foot and mouth, so all the animals on his farm will have to be slaughtered—his whole herd of lovely ruby-red Devon cows and their calves, all those sheep and lambs I saw only a couple of weeks ago. All of them are sentenced to die. It's terrible, horrible.

From my bedroom window I could see what was going on across the river. There were men in white overalls rounding up the sheep. When Mum told me they were probably the slaughterers, I closed my curtains. I won't look again. I don't want to see what happens. I don't want even to think about it. I don't want to write about it. But what else is there to think about? What else can I write about? It's in my head all the time, on the telly every time we turn it on. It's in the air I'm breathing.

Praying doesn't work. I bet Mr Bailey prayed, and I bet Terry Bolan prayed too. It didn't help them, did it? I've put disinfectant all around Little Josh's shippen like a sort of protective shield, and I never let them out now in case they breathe in the disease. The less they're outside in the fields the better. Dad's brought the whole of his flock into the lambing shed. Like he says, this virus can fly on the wind, it can come in on the birds, so he's not letting them out again. And you don't even know if sheep have got it, not for three weeks. It takes three weeks for the disease to show itself. So I won't let mine out either, no matter how much fuss Little Josh makes. I can hear him now, bleating to be let out. I've told him why he's got to stay in. I wish he could understand me as well as I understand him. I don't pray any more. I just hope and hope and hope.

THURSDAY, MARCH 8TH

My nightmare began this morning. I went out for a ride, just to give Ruby some exercise. We rode down through Bluebell Wood to the river. The river was bank high again. Ruby was drinking and I was looking up across the river at Mr Bailey's farm. It was deserted, not an animal in sight, just crows cawing over the wood, cackling at me as if they knew something I didn't. Suddenly, I knew what it was. The last time I'd ridden Ruby down to the river was before we knew about the foot and mouth. I'd crossed over on to Mr Bailey's farm. I'd galloped up through his wood and out over his sheep field. I'd been in amongst his sheep, sheep that must already have been infected with foot and mouth disease. I'd come home again bringing the foot and mouth with me on Ruby, on my clothes, in my hair. We'd come back through the river, but river water isn't disinfectant. We'd carried the germs with us back on to our farm. And I'd gone out with Dad checking the animals. I touched them. I helped him with the milking that evening. I milked Primrose myself. I fed Little Josh.

This is the worst feeling I've had in all my life. Ever since I first thought of what I might have done I've felt cold all over. I've been sick. All I know is that if it happens now, if we get foot and mouth, then it'll be all my fault.

FRIDAY, MARCH 9TH
(around 1.00 in the morning)

I can't sleep, and not just because of the dreadful thing I might have done. They've lit the fire on Terry Bolan's farm. I can see the sky glowing red from my window and I can smell it. It's the same smell the blacksmith makes when he comes to shoe Ruby, when he puts the hot-iron shoe up against Ruby's hoof to see if it fits properly and the whole stable fills with acrid smoke. I've already used up all that perfume Gran sent me for Christmas. I sprinkled it everywhere in my room so I couldn't smell the smoke, so I wouldn't be reminded all the time of what was burning. I discovered that the smell of death is stronger than perfume, and lasts longer.

Dad couldn't sleep either. I heard him going out every couple of hours to check the animals. Around midnight I decided to get up and follow him because I thought he'd like the company. I found him in with his cows, just sitting there on the edge of the water trough, watching them lying in the straw all around him and chewing the cud. Then I saw that he was crying. I've never in my life seen Dad cry before. I didn't think he could cry. I felt like going to him and putting my arms around him, but I couldn't. I couldn't because I knew he would hate me to see him like this.

And then, as I was walking away, I heard him talking, not to the cows, not to me, not to himself. He was talking to Grandad, his dad. And Grandad's dead. He died a long time ago before I was born. I know him just from photographs, from stories. He was talking to him as if he was there with him in the barn. 'Don't let it happen, Pop,' he was saying. 'Please don't let it happen. Tell me what I've got to do to stop it from happening.' I felt as if I was prying, so I crept away and left him.

I looked in on Little Josh as I passed by the shippen. He was fine, so far as I could tell. Then I came back up to my room and wrote this. A deep sadness has settled in my heart. I think it will

never go away.

SATURDAY, MARCH 10TH

I'm not at home any more. I'm at Auntie Liz's place in the village. When I woke up this morning the smell was worse than ever. It was like a fog all around the house. This time it was from Mr Bailey's farm where they started burning the animals last night. Mum said it wasn't healthy for me to stay, not until the fire had burnt itself out. I didn't want to go, but she said it would only be for a few days, and that she'd look after Little Josh and Ruby for me. So I gave in. Anyway I like going to stay with Auntie Liz.

After breakfast I went to say goodbye to Dad. He was in the dairy cutting the curd when I found him. He came and put his arms around me and held me tight as if he never wanted to let go. At that moment I wanted so much to come clean, to confess my guilty secret, that I'd ridden out on Mr Bailey's farm and might have brought the foot and mouth home with me. I knew he wouldn't blame me, but I just could not bring myself to say the words. Then I said goodbye to Ruby and Little Josh and here I am.

They're always really kind to me here. Auntie Liz fusses over me—a nice kind of fussing. But there are problems. She feeds me too much, calls me a 'growing girl.' Not what I want to hear. I don't want to grow. I'm big enough, especially my bottom. I've been trying not to eat, but I can't *not* eat at Auntie Liz's, because I love her food. Then there's Big Josh who never leaves me alone. He's sitting by me now watching me as I write. I've promised to read him a story when I've finished this. When I read he sucks his thumb and looks up into my face, never at the book. I think he likes watching my lips move. Sometimes he'll copy how I speak and break out in giggles.

You can't smell the smoke of the fires here like you can at home. But the disease is here. I can feel it all around me and so can everyone. It's like living in a ghost village, a plague village. No cars go up and down. No one's out in the street. They're all hiding behind their doors. And the birds don't sing.

There's another reason I like Auntie Liz. She says what she really feels, and most people don't. She says it'll break Dad's heart if we get foot and mouth. 'Your dad really loves his animals,' she said. 'I mean they're not just a business to him like with some farmers. They're

like family to him.' Uncle Mark said she was upsetting me, but she wasn't. She was only saying what I know already.

I rang home this evening and asked Mum how things were. She sounded strange, a bit distant. She said she was missing me, they both were, that Dad had just come in from checking the animals and they were all fine. But the

wind was still blowing the smoke from Mr Bailey's farm all around the house. It was a good thing I was away, she said. Little Josh was fine. Ruby too. I wasn't to worry about anything.

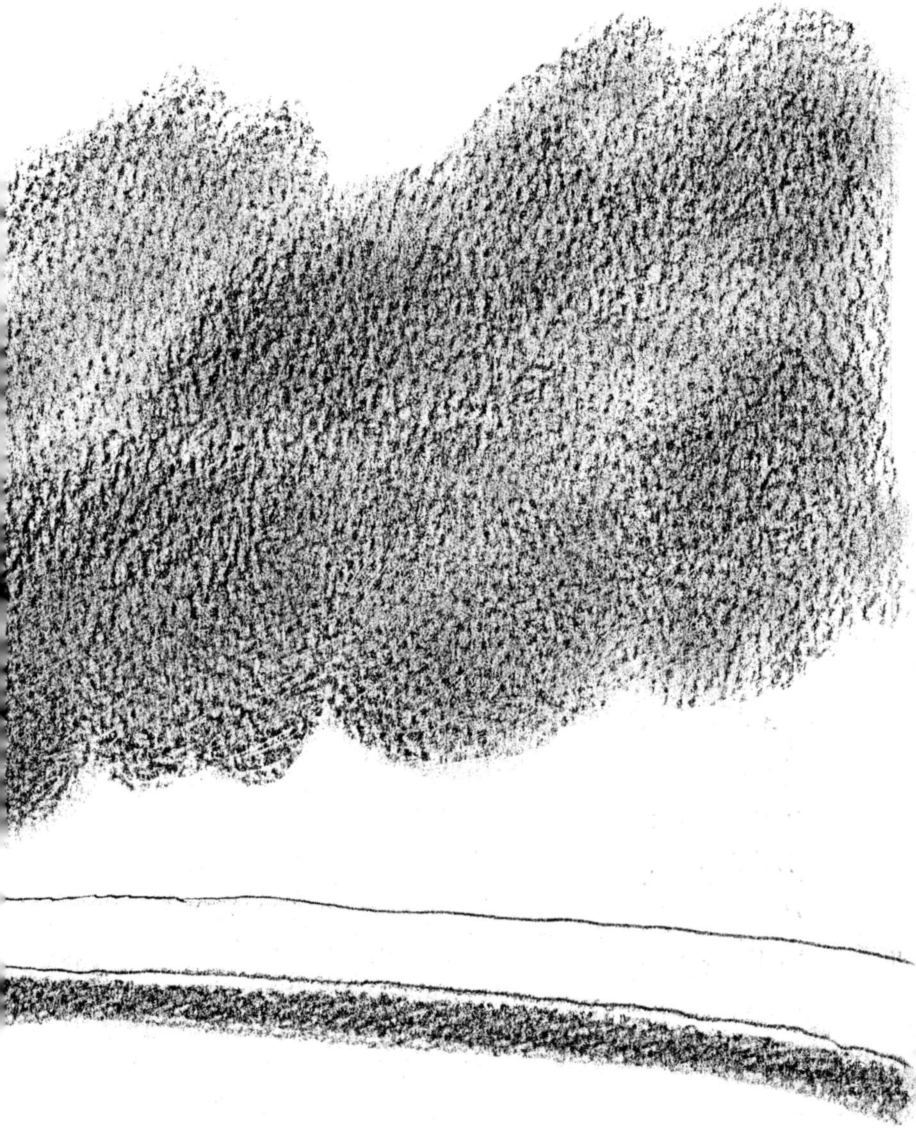

MONDAY, MARCH 12TH

I can't put into words what I feel. There are no words black enough to say what I've got to say.

We were having supper when the phone rang. Auntie Liz answered it. I knew right away something was wrong, and I knew from the moment she looked at me exactly what it was. She handed me the phone. Mum was trying not to cry as she told me. She hadn't wanted to worry me about it yesterday, she said, but the vet had been called in yesterday morning. Dad had found blisters on the feet of one of our sows, Jessica, and was worried about a couple of sheep that were limping badly. Tests had confirmed it. We had foot and mouth disease on the farm. There was an 'A' notice on the farm gate which meant no one was allowed in or out except the vets and the slaughterers. The animals would be put down tomorrow. So I'd have to stay with Auntie Liz until it was all over. It would be the best place for me, she said.

When I asked how Dad was, she said he was very calm, as if he'd been expecting it all along. She said she'd phone again tomorrow, and that she loved me. I don't remember the last time she said that to me. She sounded almost like a different person.

I've been sitting here on the bed in a daze ever since. Not crying. I can't cry. It's me who's done this, it must be. I brought the infection back with me from Mr Bailey's farm. Ruby or Bobs or me, but whichever of us it was, it had been my doing, my fault. I had sentenced our animals to death. Big Josh is sitting beside me holding my hand and he's looking so sad. I feel like he's taking the sadness out of me and into himself, leaving me numb inside. They're going to kill them all—Jemima, Jessica, Hector, Primrose, all Dad's cows, all his pigs, all his sheep, and Little Josh.

P.S. Auntie Liz put on a video, to help take my mind off things, she said.

Seven Days in Tibet with Brad Pitt. She'd chosen it specially because she knows how much I love Brad Pitt. I sat looking at the screen, but not seeing. All I could think of the whole way through was Little Josh, and tomorrow.

I want tomorrow never to come. But tomorrow always comes.

TUESDAY, MARCH 13TH

I'll never be able to think of this date without thinking of the Angels of Death. So much has happened and all of it so fast and so final. Today began yesterday. Last night after I'd finished writing my diary, I made a decision. I was lying in my bed at Auntie Liz's and thinking about Little Josh, and home and Mum and Dad. I just decided I had to go home, that I had caused this, that I had to be there with them.

I waited till everyone was in bed and asleep. I left a letter on my pillow explaining everything to Auntie Liz, telling her I was going home. Then I got dressed, packed my things, and crept downstairs. I ran out of the village, up through the graveyard and on to the footpath—no one would see me if I went that way. I thought I'd find the way home easily—I'd done it hundreds of times before—but never in the dark. As it turned out, it was a good thing that I lost my way. The footpath should have brought me out on to the road right opposite our gate, but instead I came out on the road further up. I looked back down the road towards our farm gate and there was a police car parked right across the gateway, and a policeman standing by the car smoking a cigarette. I waited until he got back in the car, then sprinted across the road and up through Front Field and home.

The lights were still on in the kitchen. Mum and Dad were sitting there at the table and talking over a cup of tea. I just walked in and told them everything. I told them that it was me who'd brought back the foot and mouth after I'd been riding on Mr Bailey's farm. I told them I was staying home no matter what. I don't know how much they understood of what I said because I was crying so much. But they understood enough. Dad held my hands and told me it was no one's fault, not mine, not anyone's. The foot and mouth disease could have come on the wind, in the smoke, on bird droppings, car tyres—a hundred different ways, he said. And Mum said I shouldn't have run away like I did, but I knew they were both really pleased I had and that neither of them blamed me at all. I could tell that from the way they hugged me. It was a strange thing to be suddenly happy in the middle of all this, but I was.

Today began again this morning. I was up early and went off to feed Little Josh, while Dad did the milking. Mum let all the ewes and lambs out into Front Field. We stood and watched them as they spread out over the field, the ewes at once busy at their grazing, the lambs springing and skipping, loving their sudden freedom, their last freedom. Neither of us said a word. We didn't need to because we were both thinking the same thoughts. Little Josh wouldn't stay with the others. He followed me home into the kitchen. So I fed him. But even when I'd fed him he wanted to stay by me.

We saw the men in white—the slaughterers and the vets—walking up the farm lane as we finished our breakfast. Dad got up, pulled on his overalls, and went out without a word. Mum cried when he'd gone. I put my arms around her and tried to comfort her, but I didn't cry. I didn't cry because my mind was on other things and it was racing. I was looking down at Little Josh lying at my feet, and I was thinking. I was thinking about how I was going to hide him away, so that the men in white would never find him. I didn't know where I would hide him, but I knew it had to be done. And it had to be soon, very soon. There wasn't much time.

My chance came when Mum got up from the table and said she just couldn't sit there and let Dad do it on his own, that she had to go with him. The moment she'd gone, I scooped Josh up into my arms and ran upstairs. I cleared out everything I could from the bottom of my cupboard and laid down some newspaper. I sat on my bed and fed him again until he couldn't drink another drop. I told him that he must be quiet, that he must go to sleep and keep quiet. He seemed happy enough—until I lifted him in and shut the cupboard door on him. Then he started, bleating on and on, like he'd never stop. It was muffled, but I could still hear him, and if I could hear him, so could they. So I put on my CD just loud enough to drown out his bleating and left him there. All I had to do now was to be sure that I kept my CD going.

Later, more slaughtermen in white arrived—'Angels of Death,' Mum called them. She came in and told me the shooting would begin very soon, that I mustn't on any account go outside from now on. She didn't have to tell me. Nothing and no one could have made me go out and watch what they'd be doing. Just thinking of it was more than I could bear. I stayed in my room behind my closed curtains, cradled Little Josh on my lap, put on my earphones and turned up my CD so loud that I couldn't hear the shooting, so that I couldn't feel or know anything except the thunder of the music in my head.

But then I had to change the CD. I took off my earphones without thinking. That was when I first heard the shooting, not loud, not near, but the crack of every shot told me that this was really happening. They were killing out there, killing Dad's family of animals.

Suddenly I thought of Ruby. She'd be frightened out of her mind at all the shooting. I put Little Josh back in the cupboard, turned up the CD, ran downstairs, and out across the yard to her stable.

Ruby was in a real state by the time I got there, all lathered up and terrified. I went in with her, closed the top of the stable door and hugged her, smoothing her, calming her all I could. After a while when the shooting stopped, she relaxed a little and rested her head on my shoulder. Even then I could hear her heart pounding as if she'd been galloping.

Then I opened the door. I wish I hadn't. Dad was there. Mum was there, her arm round his shoulder. The men in white were there. There was blood on their overalls, blood on their boots. One of them was holding a clipboard and he was the one doing the talking.

'There's no mistake, Mr Morley,' he was saying. 'I've checked this list a dozen times now and we've counted the bodies. We're one lamb missing, one ram lamb, a Suffolk.'

It's not their fault, I know, but if Mum and Dad hadn't seen me in the stable at that moment, if they hadn't looked at me like they did, no one would ever have guessed. Even Bobs was looking at me. Mum knew what I'd done the moment she caught my eye. She came over and explained that I had to give Little Josh up, had to say where he was, that every cloven-hoofed animal on the farm had to be killed. There couldn't be any exceptions. I buried my face in Ruby's neck. I was sobbing too much to say anything. I knew it was over, that it was hopeless, that sooner or later they would find him. So I told them I'd fetch him out myself. And that's what I did. I carried him out. He didn't struggle, just bleated a little as I handed him over. The man in white who took him off me had a face. It was Brad and his eyes were full of tears. 'It'll be very quick,' he said. 'He won't know anything. He won't feel anything.' And he carried him away around the back of the shed. A few moments later there was a shot. I felt it like a knife in my heart.

This evening the farm is still, is silent. The fields are empty, and it's raining.

THURSDAY, MARCH 15TH

Our farm isn't ours any more. People I don't even know come and go everywhere. They're all over the place, like ants. There's been lorries coming in and out all day, bringing in railway sleepers and straw for the fire. And there's diggers, two of them, digging the trench in Front Field. I can see them now from my window, waving their arms about like great yellow monsters, doing a hideous dance of death to the thunderous music of their engines.

The phone rings all the time, but we don't pick it up and we don't answer messages unless we have to. Auntie Liz left a message, so did Jay, so did Gran, all saying how terrible it is, how sorry they are, how they're thinking of us. Auntie Liz was in tears, and Jay says it was horrible of her to have quarrelled with me like she did that day (I'd forgotten all about it long ago) and she said how much she misses me. I miss her too—lots. Gran says she wishes she could be with us, to help us. But I'm glad she's not. Three of us being silent, being so full of sadness is enough. She'd only make it worse. Besides, we can manage on our own.

Mum sent me to the end of the lane to pick up the post and the milk this morning. The policeman was still there, still smoking. He said he was sorry too. Then he gave me a bit of a talking-to. I don't remember much of what he said, something about a light at the end of the tunnel. He was trying to be nice. And I could see he was upset for us, really upset, not pretending.

Mum says it's the first time since she's been married that she's ever had to buy milk. The post is mostly cards, most with flowers on, the kind of cards people send when someone in the family has died. The cremation will be in Front Field as soon as they've built the funeral pyre.

The burning can't come too soon for any of us. There's already a horrible stench about the place. Mum said I mustn't go near the sheds where they killed the cows and the pigs, nor out into the Front Field where the sheep are lying. She doesn't want me to see them. And I don't want to see them either. Imagining them is bad enough. Most of the day Dad sits at his desk smoking and saying nothing. There's no work for him to do any more. No milking. No feeding the animals. No cheesemaking. He hasn't been back into his cheese store to check the cheese. I don't think he can bear to look at them.

FRIDAY, MARCH 16TH

Tonight when Dad didn't come in for tea I was worried, and I went out to look for him. I heard him before I found him. He was in with the cows in the barn, sitting on a bale of hay, with his head in his hands. Hector was lying at his feet. Dad was talking to Grandad just like he had before. I remember exactly the words he said: 'Tell me why, Pop. Tell me why. Will you tell me what I've done to deserve this?'

His cows lay all about him, with their eyes staring, stiffened and swollen in death, and everywhere a terrible stillness. Mum was right. I shouldn't have gone. I shouldn't have seen what I've seen. It'll be locked in my head for ever.

MONDAY, MARCH 19TH

Yesterday evening they lit the fire at last. I looked out of my window and remembered the last bonfire we'd had on the farm, on Front Field in about the same place. It was Millennium night, and everyone had come and we'd had sausages and cake and cider. And Dad had sung 'Danny Boy,' because everyone had asked him to. It's his favourite song in the world. This is a very different sort of a fire. This one belches out clouds of horrible stinking smoke, and it will burn for days, they tell us. But then it'll all be over. I'm longing for that, longing for the smoke and the smell to be gone, for us to be left alone, for the pain to be over.

On the television there are always more and more cases, two more in the village, Barrow Farm and Fursdon. If it goes on like this there'll be no farm animals left.

It's strange how you can get used to things though—even to a nightmare.

We've been trapped on the farm, quarantined, forbidden to leave for nearly a week now, but I wouldn't want to leave even if I could. I spend my days mostly with Ruby and Bobs. Except for the hens and the ducks, they're the only animals left alive on the farm. I go riding along the water meadows as far as I can from the smoke, and from the men in white overalls.

This morning I saw Mr Bailey down there doing some fencing. We waved at each other. I couldn't hear what he said at first, but then he shouted it again. 'I said, don't you worry, girl. Things'll look up, you'll see,' He's been more

friendly since foot and mouth than he ever was before. He's sent a card, and he's rung up too, offering to come over and give a hand. I told Mum and Dad about what Mr Bailey had said because I thought it might cheer them up a bit—I don't think either of them even heard me. Living with Mum and Dad is like living with ghosts—sad, silent ghosts. Mum doesn't cry any more. Dad does, not in front of me, but I hear him in the bedroom. I can hear him now as I'm writing this.

SUNDAY, MARCH 25TH

The fire is out, and the people are gone. It's done. It's over. I talked to Jay on the phone again today. She's been ringing a lot in the last few days. It's been really good to talk to her. She never talks about foot and mouth. She's the only reminder I've got that there are other things happening out there. I'm still quarantined, still not allowed out, not allowed back at school. This morning she told me that everyone in my class has written to me and that, if I liked, she could bring the letters to the farm gate after school and hand them over.

So we met up this afternoon at the end of the farm lane. She looked the same. I don't know why, but I expected her to be different. We chatted for a long time. It was difficult at first, like we were strangers almost—even though we've spoken often on the phone. She gave me all the hot gossip. Apparently Sally Burton's boasting that she's going out with Peter Mitchum, who's now got a Mohican haircut and fancies himself rotten, but Jay knows for a fact that Peter is already going out with Linda Morrish. I laughed, not just because she laughed, but because it sounded like news from another planet. Then she handed me this huge brown envelope with all the letters from school. She told me that Mrs Merton had been in tears when she heard about our farm, and that she'd written a letter to me too. It was great seeing Jay again, hearing her voice. For a short time I was part of the world again, the world outside. I watched her cycle off until she disappeared round the corner, and then suddenly I felt very alone.

I've been sitting on my bed reading the letters from school again and again. Some were written to all of us, to Mum and Dad and me, but most just to me.

Mrs Merton wrote this: 'It must all seem very grim and hopeless at the moment. But you mustn't lose heart. You tell your family that we're thinking of them, and that one day soon all this

misery will be over. There'll be animals on the farm, and life will be as it was once again. There will be a life for you all after foot and mouth, and a good life too.'

The church bells are ringing. Someone else must be ringing Dad's bell.

WEDNESDAY, MARCH 28TH

I've never been ill, not seriously ill, just colds and toothache. But I think this is like being really ill, so ill you can't forget it for a single moment. And the illness has changed everything. None of us can do what we used to do. Mum can't go to work at her school, I still can't go to my school nor see my friends, Dad can't milk his cows nor make his cheese.

Our fire may be out, but when I looked out of the window first thing this morning I could see the smoke from three fires drifting down the valley. It's like the whole world is sick. And Dad is trying to wash it away. He's out there from dawn to dusk working like a madman. Ever since the ministry told him that every building on the farm has to be cleared out and disinfected, he hasn't stopped. He's out there now—and it's nearly nine o'clock at night—cleaning off the rafters in the lambing shed. He's been at it all day.

Mum has tried to stop him, to slow him down. But he won't listen. I told Mum today how I'd heard him talking to Grandad in the cow barn. She looked very worried, but then she told me something that explained it a bit. Apparently it was in the cow barn that Grandad had died all those years before. He was feeding the cows one day and just dropped dead of a heart attack. Mum said it was the smell of the dead animals that upset Dad, that made him work like he was. He just wants to get rid of the smell.

Mum and I are better together than we've ever been before. There's no pretending any more, on either side. Before this I never really thought of her as a person, just Mum, Mum pestering me, Mum organizing me, organizing Dad. But she's not like that now. She cries like I do. I think she really needs me, as much as I need her.

Mum and I went down to the farm gate to get our shopping. Auntie Liz brings it out to us every other day. Big Josh was with her—he likes me calling him 'Big Josh'. He asked me if I'd got ‘leg and mouth’, and we laughed. I just wanted to hug him, he’s so sweet! I couldn’t hug him or even touch him just in case I’ve got the virus on me somewhere. So I blew him a kiss over the gate and he blew me loads back.

I think all the time about Little Josh. I see him as I saw him for the last time being carried off, still bleating. Was he crying out for help? Was he saying goodbye? Did he know what was happening? I hope not.

I dreamed about Hector last night. I can’t remember all of it, only that he came into the barn and bellowed, and all the cows rose from the dead and followed him out into the field. And Dad was there, laughing like he used to.

FRIDAY, MARCH 30TH

On the way back from the farm gate with the shopping this afternoon we saw Dad out on Front Field. He was standing by the mass grave. He had a single daffodil in his hand. Suddenly he just fell on his knees and began crying. Mum and I ran to him, and took him home. He cried into his hat all the way. Mum sat him down in the kitchen, and talked to him, but he couldn't stop crying. I came up here to my room. It's like foot and mouth isn't satisfied with killing all our animals. It's killing Dad too.

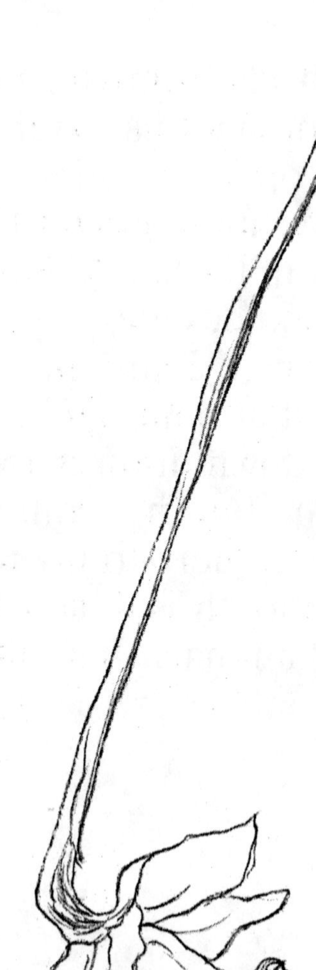

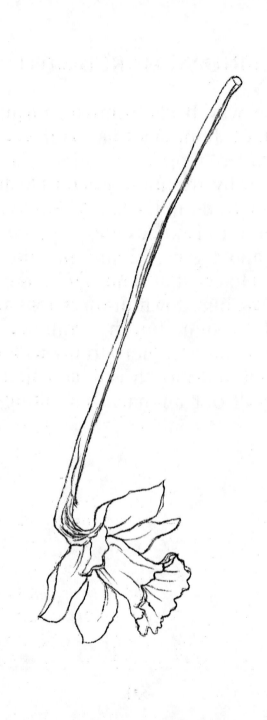

THURSDAY, APRIL 5TH

I thought after the fire had burnt itself out that the worst would be over. I was wrong.

When we woke up this morning Dad was gone. We looked everywhere, but we couldn't find him. I noticed the Land-Rover was gone, and then Mum discovered his shotgun was gone too. She called the police. After that we sat at the kitchen table and waited. Mum said she knew she should have made him see a doctor, that she knew he wasn't well. He hadn't been eating. He hadn't been sleeping. All he did was scrub the sheds and cry. She kept blaming herself, and I kept saying it would be all right, that Dad would come home, that he'd be fine. But I didn't believe it. Every hour we waited there in the kitchen seemed like a day. Both of us thought the worst—that he'd gone off somewhere and killed himself—but neither of us dared say it.

We sat by the phone all day just

holding hands, hoping and praying and crying. And then this evening we had the phone call. They've found him. He was out at Stoke Church in Hartland, sitting by Grandad's grave. He was very upset and very confused, they said. They've taken him to North Devon Hospital at Barnstaple, and he's been given some pills to help him sleep. He's fine. We can go in and see him tomorrow.

So the worst wasn't the worst. Some prayers do work after all.

FRIDAY, APRIL 6TH

I hate hospitals. I hate the look of them. I hate the smell of them. Lying in a huge hospital bed Dad looked very small and sunken and sleepy. When I gave him his bananas—he loves bananas—he tried his best to smile, but it very soon turned to tears. He kept saying over and over again that he was sorry and that he shouldn't have gone off like he had, that he didn't know what he was doing.

We didn't stay long, so as not to tire him, and then Mum went off to see the doctor and left me outside in the corridor. She told me what they'd said on the way home in the car, that Dad's not likely to be out of hospital for at least a couple of weeks. He's depressed, badly depressed. It's not something Dad ever liked to talk about, she said, but he had been depressed once before when he was much younger. And depression isn't just sadness, she told me. It's an illness

that makes you feel very bad about yourself, that makes you feel completely useless and lost, as if you're living at the bottom of a deep dark pit of hopelessness that you can see no way out of. They're giving Dad medication and treatment to make him feel better, and he'll be seeing a psychiatrist to help him come to terms with everything that's happened, but it might be a long time before he's completely better.

I think Mum and I talked more about Dad on the way home today than we ever have before; but not like mother and daughter, more like best friends holding hands through a nightmare we long to wake up from, but can't. We know that all we've got now is each other.

SUNDAY, APRIL 22ND

Dad's still in hospital. I really miss him being about the place. Mum goes in to see him every day after work, and I go with her at weekends. Today, for the first time, he seems more like his old self. He was still a bit sleepy, but the crying has stopped. He even laughs a little. He's been doing a few sketches each day, to stop himself from going mad with boredom, he said. He didn't want to show me at first, but I bullied him till he did. He's done pages and pages of lovely pen portraits of the animals that died, Hector, Jessica, Molly—every one of them, with their names underneath each one. 'It's so's I don't forget them,' he told me. He didn't seem at all sad when he said it, just matter of fact. He's so much better, but I've noticed that he drifts away from us sometimes into his own thoughts, into a world of his own. A shadow seems to fall over him, but then it passes and he's back with us again.

He says the food in hospital is horrible. His friend in the bed next to his says they all call him 'chimp' on the ward, because he only eats bananas.

Best of all, he's making plans for the future, and when he talks about it he's really excited. He says he can't wait to get back home. He wants to get the farm ready for when he buys in a new herd of Gloucester cows. We're not allowed to have animals on the place for another five months. He's already got the compensation money, but he's going to start slowly, he says. He reckons in a year or so the farm'll be 'just like it was, I promise'. And there was a real sparkle in his eye when he said it.

Mrs Merton was right in her letter—there is going to be life after foot and mouth.

(Dad's drawings, not mine)

Rose
May
Tulip
Molly
Jemima

FRIDAY, APRIL 27TH

Everyone's saying that the worst of the foot and mouth is over now. There are still a few cases each week, most of them up north, but none around here. And for the first time this morning when I went down the road to catch the school bus, I couldn't smell the fires. And the birds were singing.

I'm back at school now—have been for a few days. I felt a bit out of place at first. No one seemed to know what to say to me, except Jay. She's been great. She's the only one I've told about Dad—that's because I really know I can trust her. Most people at school don't live on farms, so they only know what it's been like from the television. They know the animals are killed and burnt, but they don't know how it affects people, the farmers, the families. It's not their fault. How could they know? And then today, Mrs Merton asked everyone in the class to think up questions to ask me about how it had been, about what had happened on the farm, about the animals. (She'd spoken to me first. I was a bit nervous about it, but it seemed like a good idea so I agreed.) When I told them about Little Josh I could feel the sadness and the stillness in the room around me. It felt right to talk about it, to tell them about Little Josh and Molly and Jessica and Hector. And I didn't cry once, not so that anyone could see or hear anyway.

When I got off the bus this afternoon and walked up the lane I saw there were swallows swooping over the fields, and primroses in the hedgerows, and the bees were out, and there was warmth on the back of my neck and in my heart too. All the trees that were winter-dead are alive again and green with leaves.

Dad's coming home soon, probably next Monday. I can't wait. I can't wait to see his face when he sees what we've done.

MONDAY, APRIL 30TH

Mum went off early to fetch Dad back from the hospital. Everything worked out just as we had planned it. I was waiting in the yard as the Land-Rover drove in.

'Come and see,' I said, and I took his hand and led him round. The whole yard, all the sheds and shippens and barns were all cleaned out and spotless. No muck, no smell, no reminders. Dad beamed as he looked about him. And then I told him how it had been Uncle Mark's idea to get the place all tidied up and ready for him when he came home, and how Uncle Mark and Auntie Liz and Big Josh had come to stay over Easter to help out, and how Mr Bailey had lent a hand as well. Dad shook his head in disbelief and then went off on his own into the cow barn for a while. When he came out, he said, 'It's like it's all waiting, isn't it? Waiting for a new chapter to begin.'

Afterwards

On October 5th (Dad's birthday!), six new Gloucester cows arrived, four of them already in milk with calves at foot, and Dad started milking again and making his cheese.

On October 30th when I got back from school I found a new flock of twenty-five ewes, Cotswolds again, out in Front Field. The grass has grown over the grave site now—you'd hardly know it was there. We've planted an oak tree at the far end of it in memory of Little Josh and Hector and all of them. It'll grow out of the ashes and be there for hundreds of years.

And today it's November 5th, and the pigs have arrived. Just three, but as Dad says: 'With pigs, three soon becomes thirty.' They're all Gloucester Old Spots. The boar we've called Guy, and his two sows are Geraldine and Georgia. They're gorgeous!

It's half-term and Dad's finally stopped smoking. I was out riding Ruby

this morning with Bobs trotting along beside us when I saw Dad out on his tractor. He was ploughing in Drot Field up against Bluebell Wood. He came closer and closer, looking back over his shoulder from time to time at the plough. He didn't notice we were there. And, as he came past he was singing. He was singing 'Danny Boy' at the top of his voice.

Author's Note

In the last few months, foot and mouth has spread like wildfire through our countryside. Thousands of farming families have seen their life's work destroyed before their eyes as over three million animals have been slaughtered. It has been an unimaginable catastrophe.

It was to reflect the impact of this tragedy that I wrote *Out of the Ashes*. The story in itself is not true but has been woven together from events that I know to be true or have witnessed myself.

Michael Morpurgo
Iddesleigh, Devon
June 2001

www.outoftheashes.co.uk

If you have been affected by the foot and mouth outbreak and have stories of your own experiences to tell, you can post them at this website.